ANDREW LOST

7

ON THE REEF

BY J. C. GREENBURG

ILLUSTRATED
BY JAN GERARDI

A STEPPING STONE BOOK™

Random House 🏠 New York

To Dan and Zack and Dad
and the real Andrew, with love.
And to Jim Thomas, Mallory Loehr,
and all my Random House friends,
with an ocean of thanks.
—J.C.G.

Text copyright © 2004 by J. C. Greenburg. Illustrations copyright
© 2004 by Jan Gerardi. All rights reserved under International and
Pan-American Copyright Conventions. Published in the United
States by Random House Children's Books, a division of Random
House, Inc., New York, and simultaneously in Canada by Random
House of Canada Limited, Toronto.

www.randomhouse.com/kids
www.AndrewLost.com

Library of Congress Cataloging-in-Publication Data
Greenburg, J. C. (Judith C.)
On the reef / by J. C. Greenburg ; illustrated by Jan Gerardi. — 1st ed.
   p.   cm. — (Andrew Lost ; 7)
"A stepping stone book."
SUMMARY: After escaping from the belly of a whale, Andrew and his
cousin Judy face more dangers from their underwater nemesis,
Soggy Bob, in the Great Barrier Reef.
ISBN 0-375-82525-8 (trade) — ISBN 0-375-92525-2 (lib. bdg.)
[1. Marine animals—Fiction. 2. Inventions—Fiction.
3. Cousins—Fiction.]   I. Gerardi, Jan, ill.   II. Title.
III. Series: Greenburg, J. C. (Judith C.), Andrew Lost ; v 7.
PZ7.G82785   Op   2004   [Fic]—dc21   2003009681

Printed in the United States of America
First Edition 10 9 8 7 6

RANDOM HOUSE and colophon are registered trademarks and A STEPPING
STONE BOOK and colophon are trademarks of Random House, Inc.
ANDREW LOST is a trademark of J. C. Greenburg.

CONTENTS

ANDREW'S WORLD

Andrew Dubble

Andrew is ten years old, but he's been inventing things since he was four. Some of his inventions have gotten him into trouble, like the time he shrunk himself, his cousin Judy, and his little silver robot Thudd smaller than the foot of a flea with the Atom Sucker.

Andrew is in hot water again. He fooled around with his Uncle Al's underwater vehicle, the Water Bug. Now Andrew, Judy, and Thudd are about to meet some of the most dangerous creatures on earth!

Judy Dubble

Judy is Andrew's thirteen-year-old cousin. She thought she was too smart to let Andrew drag her into another crazy adventure. But that was before he showed her the Water Bug. . . . Now she's busy trying to save giant squids!

Thudd

The Handy Ultra-Digital Detective. Thudd is a super-smart robot and Andrew's best friend. This hasn't been an easy trip for Thudd. He's a little worried about what's next!

Uncle Al

Andrew and Judy's uncle is a top-secret scientist. He invented Thudd and the Water Bug. Uncle Al is worried about Andrew, Judy, and Thudd. He's finishing up a new underwater vehicle called the See Horse so that he can rescue them!

The Water Bug

It used to be an old Volkswagen Beetle until Uncle Al turned it into a submarine. Now it has a glass floor, a sharky fin on its roof, and a bathroom in the backseat. Andrew, Judy, and Thudd are pretty safe when they're inside it. Too bad it's trapped on the ocean floor!

Soggy Bob Sloggins

This bad guy of the sea is building Animal Universe, the biggest theme park in the world. But Soggy Bob doesn't care about the animals. He hung a sign above the aquarium in Squid World. It says SOGGY BOB'S GIANT SQUIDWICHES—COMING SOON!

Now Soggy Bob is after Andrew, Judy, and Thudd, too. Will they be able to stop Soggy Bob from turning giant squids into giant snacks? Or will Soggy Bob get them into the biggest Dubble trouble ever?

TRAPPED!

Now I know what it feels like to be a fish! thought Andrew Dubble.

That was because Andrew's underwater vehicle, the Water Bug, was tangled in a huge net at the bottom of the ocean.

On the other side of the net were craggy mountains of coral and fish that looked like slices of a rainbow.

"Cheese Louise!" said Andrew's thirteen-year-old cousin, Judy. She was sitting next to Andrew in the passenger seat. "Maybe Soggy Bob set a trap to keep us from getting to the giant squids first!"

Soggy Bob Sloggins wanted to capture a giant squid and turn it into giant squid-wiches. Andrew and Judy were trying to stop him.

"Maybe the Water Bug can rip through the net," said Andrew. He pushed the gas pedal to the floor. *VROOOOOOOM!*

The Water Bug used to be a Volkswagen Beetle. It had a glass floor, a sharky fin on its roof, and a bathroom in the backseat!

The Water Bug whammed into the net, bounced off, and thumped into the ocean floor. Now the Water Bug's paddle wheels were caught in the net!

A herd of tiny yellow box-shaped fish fluttered up to the windshield. Their big blue eyes peered in curiously at Andrew and Judy.

meep . . . "Try Octo-Tool," came a squeaky voice. It was Andrew's little silver robot and best friend, Thudd. He was sitting in a pocket of Andrew's underwater suit.

"Good idea, Thudd," said Andrew.

He pressed a black button on the dashboard.

"Untangle Water Bug," said Andrew into a microphone near the steering wheel.

glurp . . . "Will try," came the voice of the Water Bug.

The hood of the Water Bug popped open and the gray tentacles of the Octo-Tool slithered out. They snatched at the net and tugged.

But the Water Bug wasn't coming free. Instead, the Octo-Tool's tentacles got tangled in the net, too!

glurp . . . "Alert! Alert!" said the Water Bug. "Octo-Tool trouble. Tentacles trapped!"

"Uh-oh," said Andrew. "Looks like we'll have to get out and do it ourselves."

Judy groaned. "Cheese Louise! The last time we left the Water Bug, we got swallowed by a whale!"

Andrew wasn't listening to her. "While we're out there," he said, "we can get the lava boogers out of the Super-Sniffer."

On the hood of the Water Bug was a nose-like invention called the Super-Sniffer. It tracked things in the water the way a dog tracks things on land, by smell. Andrew and Judy needed the Super-Sniffer to find the giant squids. They had to get to them before Soggy Bob!

But the Super-Sniffer was clogged up with lava boogers from an underwater volcano.

"Look!" said Andrew. He pointed to a part of the net ahead of them. It was squirming. "Something else is caught in the net."

meep . . . "Lotsa animals get caught in old fishing net," said Thudd. "Seals. Turtles. Dolphins."

Judy's eyes got wide. "You mean a dolphin could be trapped in there?" she said.

"Yoop! Yoop! Yoop!" said Thudd.

Judy sighed. "We've got to get out there right away and see what it is."

Judy and Andrew pulled their Bubble Duds helmets over their heads. Their Bubble Duds were bumpy green suits that let Andrew and Judy breathe underwater. There were headphones inside the helmets that let them talk to each other, too.

Andrew made sure Thudd's Bubble Bag was tightly closed. Thudd was never supposed

to get wet! Then Andrew sealed Thudd inside a front pocket of his Bubble Duds.

Andrew and Judy pressed buttons on the sides of their seats.

FLAMP!

Their seats flipped over, and they popped outside the Water Bug.

Peering through the green water, Andrew saw that the net was drooping from strange tall shapes. They reminded him of the ribs of a dinosaur.

Andrew and Judy swam over to the squirming bundle in the tangled net.

Suddenly Judy stopped.

"Wait a minute," she said. "What if it's a shark?"

UM, MERMAID?

"We'll have to be careful," said Andrew.

The bundle was as big as a basketball player—a very *fat* basketball player. Little by little, Andrew and Judy tugged the net away from it.

The first thing they saw was a flopping tail. It looked like a big gray Ping-Pong paddle!

"That's not a shark tail," said Judy.

meep . . . "Manatee tail!" said Thudd. "Manatee called sea cow. Eat lotsa grass. Look!"

Thudd's face screen flashed a picture of an

animal that looked like a lumpy beach toy.

"Oh!" said Judy, pulling the net away from a flapping flipper. "A long time ago, sailors thought manatees were mermaids! Manatees are gentle and sweet!"

"Maybe," said Andrew. "But a manatee sure doesn't look like a pretty girl with long hair and a fish tail."

He dragged the net away from a chubby face with tiny round eyes.

"It looks more like a baked potato with flippers," he said.

meep . . . "Manatee mammal, like dolphin," said Thudd. "Gotta breathe. Soon."

"Let's hurry," said Judy. "At the count of three, pull your end of the net, Andrew. One. Two. *Three!*"

"Erggh!" said Judy.

"Woofers!" said Andrew.

Finally, the manatee was free. It nodded its pudgy head, paddled its flippers, and circled up into the water. But it couldn't find a way through the net!

"We have to find a hole in the net," said Andrew.

Judy shook her head. "We need to cut through it," she said. "I'll see what I can find in the Water Bug."

meep . . . "Gotta hurry!" said Thudd. "Not much time left for manatee!"

Andrew swam along the net, searching

desperately for a hole. Judy scuffled quickly toward the Water Bug, kicking up silvery puffs of sand with every step.

Then Judy noticed the top of a brown bottle sticking out of the sand. She leaned over and pulled it up.

Craaaack!

It broke. Judy was holding half a bottle. She used a shell to dig up the other half, then carefully picked it up.

"Andrew!" Judy yelled as she scurried back toward the manatee. She handed Andrew half of the broken bottle. The edges were jagged and sharp.

"Be super careful," she said, "but start chopping the net!"

Judy and Andrew began hacking away. Soon they had cut a big hole.

The manatee seemed to understand. It came up to the opening in the net and swam through.

Andrew and Judy watched the chubby creature paddle toward the surface.

"Yay!" said Andrew. "We saved the manatee!"

Judy smiled.

Andrew looked closely at the broken bottle in his hand. The glass was thick and wavy. There were bubbles in it. Seashells were stuck to it.

"This doesn't look like the glass bottles you get at the store," said Andrew.

meep . . . "Bottle old, old, old!" said Thudd. "Maybe two hundred years!"

"How do you know?" asked Andrew.

meep . . . "Bubbles in glass," said Thudd. "Old bottle made by blowing hot glass. Glass blower stick hot glass lump at end of pipe, then blow glass like bubble gum."

Thudd pointed to the huge bony shapes that surrounded them. "This bottle come from old shipwreck," he said.

"Wowzers schnauzers!" said Andrew. "Maybe it's a pirate ship!"

"Or maybe it's an explorer's ship!" said Judy.

"Let's see what we can find," said Andrew.

"First things first," said Judy. "We need to get the Water Bug untangled and unclog the Super-Sniffer."

"I guess you're right," said Andrew.

Andrew set to work untangling the net from the Octo-Tool tentacles. Judy cut the net away from the Water Bug's paddle wheels.

Then Andrew reached into a pocket and pulled out the Nose Pick, a fuzzy finger on a handle.

"I'll get those lava boogers," he said.

• Andrew poked around inside the Super-Sniffer and dug out three rough black stones.

"Got 'em!" Andrew announced. "Now the Super-Sniffer should be able to pick up the trail of the giant squid."

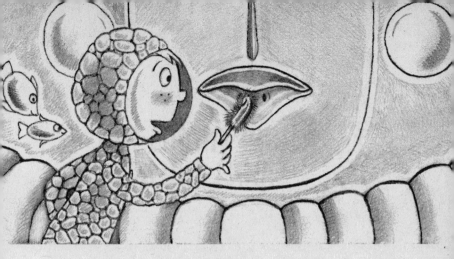

"We'd better leave fast," said Judy. "Before Soggy Bob finds us again."

"But we can't go without exploring the shipwreck," said Andrew. "I think I see something!"

Near one of the ship's ribs, a ray of light glinted off the sand. Andrew scurried over and pulled up a small round case made of metal. It had a lid that was stuck shut. Andrew pried the lid open with a shell.

"Neato mosquito!" he said. "Look what I found. It's an old compass!"

meep . . . "Purple button blinking!" squeaked Thudd. "Unkie Al coming!"

BAD THINGS IN SMALL PACKAGES

Thudd's purple button popped open and a purple hologram of Uncle Al zoomed out.

Andrew and Judy's Uncle Al was a top-secret scientist. He'd invented the Water Bug—and Thudd!

"Hey, guys!" said the Uncle Al hologram.

"So glad you're back, Uncle Al!" said Andrew, slipping the compass into a pocket.

"You've been gone a long time!" said Judy.

meep . . . "Hiya, Unkie," said Thudd.

Uncle Al was smiling, but his eyebrows were scrunched together in a worried look.

"Have you, um, gotten out of the whale yet?" he asked.

When Uncle Al visited them by hologram, he could hear them but not see them.

Judy rolled her eyes. "We sure did," she said.

"We, uh, got pooped out," said Andrew.

"That's *great,*" said Uncle Al. His smile stretched across his face.

"*Great?*" said Judy.

Uncle Al shrugged. "It's a lot better than not getting out at all," he said. "But where are you now?"

Andrew brushed away a purple-striped fish nibbling on the knee of his Bubble Duds.

"The Water Bug got trapped in a fishing net," he said. "We're outside untangling it. It looks like we're near a coral reef."

Something that looked like a baseball swam up to Andrew's face mask. It had eight little tentacles.

"Wowzers!" said Andrew. "That's weird!"

"What is?" asked Uncle Al.

"It's a tiny little octopus," said Andrew.

"Look!" said Judy. "It's got beautiful blue rings. They're flickering like a neon sign!"

"Good golly, Miss Molly!" yelled Uncle Al. "That's a blue-ringed octopus! Move away from it. *Now!*"

Andrew ducked.

Judy crossed her arms. "What's the big deal about a cute little octopus?" she asked.

Uncle Al's eyebrows wiggled up his forehead like fuzzy caterpillars.

"Judy, that cute little octopus is *deadly!*" said Uncle Al.

"Bizarre-o!" said Judy, backing away.

"Where's the octopus now?" asked Uncle Al.

"It's circling around us," said Andrew, "like a fly looking for a place to land."

"Do you see any shells or small stones?" asked Uncle Al.

Andrew picked up the lava boogers he had removed from the Super-Sniffer.

"Got some," said Andrew.

"Throw them as far as you can," said Uncle Al.

Andrew threw them one at a time. The octopus followed!

"The octopus is going after them!" said Andrew.

"Great!" said Uncle Al. "The octopus probably thinks they're clams or mussels. It likes to eat them."

Uncle Al rubbed his chin. "The good thing about the blue-ringed octopus is that it tells me where you are," he said. "Those deadly little guys live around the Great Barrier Reef. It's a coral reef near the eastern coast of Australia."

meep . . . "Great Barrier Reef more than one thousand miles long!" said Thudd. "Made by lotsa tiny coral animals. Great Barrier Reef biggest thing ever made by animal!"

"Wowzers!" said Andrew. "We were inside the blue whale, the biggest animal that ever

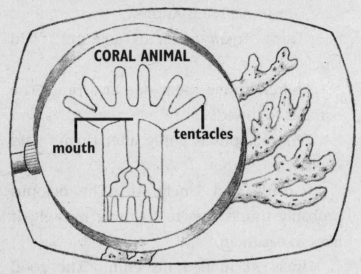

lived. Now we're right next to the biggest thing that animals ever made!"

Uncle Al nodded. "The Great Barrier Reef is a strange and beautiful place. It's also home to the most dangerous animals on earth! Danger comes in small packages there. And sometimes you can't see it at all."

"Huh?" said Judy.

"Well," said Uncle Al, "blue-ringed octopuses are hard to see. They can be as small as
Ping-Pong balls, and they don't show their
beautiful blue rings until they get mad! Then
it's too late."

"'Too late'?" asked Judy.

"Like all octopuses," said Uncle Al, "our
blue-ringed friends have sharp, parrot-like
beaks. They could bite right through your
Bubble Duds! The poison in their saliva can
kill a person in minutes. So rule number one
is never make a blue-ringed octopus mad."

"But I didn't do anything to get it mad,"
said Andrew.

Uncle Al scratched his head. "That's
strange," he said. "There are other creatures
to watch out for too, like the—"

meep . . . "Sea wasp jellyfish!" Thudd
interrupted.

"Ah, yes," said Uncle Al. "If there was a
contest for the most dangerous creature on

earth, the sea wasp would win. It's a small, box-shaped jellyfish with tentacles fifteen feet long. Its sting can kill a person in seconds!"

meep . . . "Sea wasp clear like glass," said Thudd. "Hard to see. But Bubble Duds protect Drewd and Oody from sea wasp."

"Yes," said Uncle Al. "But if there's even a tiny hole in your Bubble Duds, you could get stung. And please, please do not touch any—"

kk . . . *kkk* . . . *kkkkk* came a scratchy sound through Andrew's and Judy's headphones.

The Uncle Al hologram started spinning. It shrank down to a tiny dot and disappeared.

"Well, I'll be a bullfrog's brother!" growled a voice through their headphones. "It's those Dubble brats again!"

"Oh no!" said Judy. "It's Soggy Bob!"

CLACK! CLACK! CLACK!

Andrew saw a silvery streak coming toward them. It was Soggy Bob's underwater vehicle, the Crab-Mobile!

"Get into the Water Bug, Judy!" said Andrew.

Andrew and Judy swam to the underside of the Water Bug and pressed the buttons under the seats.

FLAMP! The seats flipped out.

Andrew and Judy strapped themselves in and pressed the buttons on the sides of the seats.

FLAMP! They flipped back into the Water Bug.

glurp . . . "Just in time," said the Water Bug.

Andrew pushed the gas pedal all the way to the floor and felt the paddle wheels start to spin. The Water Bug began to pull itself out of the sand.

Clack! Clack! Clack!

The claws of the Crab-Mobile were cutting through the net above them!

The Water Bug zoomed forward and sped through the hole they had made for the manatee. But before they could get away, a door at the front of the Crab-Mobile slid open. A big black suction cup on a thick black cord shot out!

BOINGGGG! It stuck to the hood of the Water Bug. Andrew and Judy slammed against their seats. Then—*WHAM!*—the Water Bug snapped forward.

"Woofers!" said Andrew.

"Errrgh!" said Judy. "It feels like someone's

playing volleyball with my stomach!"

PLUUUUMP!

The Water Bug's rubber-blubber buggy bumper bounced into the front of the Crab-Mobile. Its glass dome was right in front of them!

Inside they could see the shiny bald head of Soggy Bob Sloggins. His thin lips were twisted into a nasty smile.

Awk! Awk! Awk! came the mocking laugh of Bob's Ultra-Robot Parrot Partner, Burpp. He was flapping his wings on the back of Soggy Bob's zebra-striped chair. Andrew and

Judy heard the rustle of Burpp's blue metal feathers.

"Hope ya like mah No-Go Yo-Yo!" said Soggy Bob happily.

Ever since he had attacked the Water Bug with his electrical eel, Soggy Bob could talk to Andrew and Judy whenever he wanted to. But they couldn't talk back.

"Ah gotcha now, ya mud puppies!" snickered Soggy Bob. "Some friends of mine are gonna baby-sit ya while ah go huntin' that giant squid!"

Soggy Bob pulled a big red handle. A rope at the back of the Crab-Mobile towed something closer. It was a metal cage with thick bars. Inside the cage were three big gray sharks. They were chewing on the bars of the cage.

"These little fellas are a touch grouchy," said Soggy Bob. "They're losin' their baby teeth! Heh! Heh! Heh!"

Clack! Clack! Clack!

The Crab-Mobile's claws were moving toward the Water Bug's doors.

"Soggy Bob is going to pull our doors off!" said Judy.

Andrew pressed the black Octo-Tool button. But the hood of the Water Bug wouldn't open.

glurp . . . "Suction cup has sealed hood of Water Bug shut," said the Water Bug.

"Uh-oh!" said Andrew. "We've got to get out of here, Judy!"

They pressed the buttons on the sides of their seats and—

FLAMP!

They flipped out into the water again.

"I've got an idea," said Judy. "Follow me." She darted toward the bright patchwork colors of the coral reef.

Clack! Clack! Clack!

One of the Crab-Mobile's claws clamped

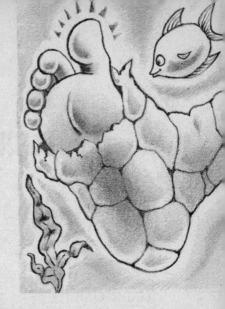

on to Andrew's toe!

"Yeoouch!" he yelled. Andrew tugged his foot away. A piece of Bubble Duds tore off, but his toes were still there.

Judy was disappearing into a crack in the high wall of the coral reef. Andrew swam faster than he ever had to catch up with her.

Inside, the walls of the reef rose like a narrow canyon. Andrew could see the surface of the water far above. In some places, coral made bridges across the canyon.

"*HELP!*" yelled Judy from farther inside the reef. "It's got my leg! I'm being eaten by a . . ."

CLAMMING UP!

"Giant clam!"

Andrew swam around a bend, and there was Judy. One of her legs was trapped between two huge shells. The top of each shell was covered with rubbery blue skin.

Clack! Clack! Clack!

Judy looked frightened.

"Don't worry about the Crab-Mobile," said Andrew. "It's way too big to get in here."

kk . . . kkk . . . kkkkk . . .

"If ya mud puppies think ya got away," growled Soggy Bob through their headphones, "ah've got some big little surprises waitin' for ya!"

Awk! "Burpp gets to ride in the Egg-Mobile!" squawked the parrot.

Judy pounded her fists on the clamshell. "Help me get out of this stupid clam! *Now!*"

Judy pushed one lip of the clamshell and Andrew pulled the other. But the clam wouldn't budge.

"Whew!" said Andrew. "This is an awfully strong clam."

meep . . . "Got idea," said Thudd from the pocket of Andrew's Bubble Duds. He pointed to little black spots on the edge of the clam's bright blue skin.

"Giant clam got eyes," said Thudd. "Can see light and dark. When giant clam see Oody's shadow, it close shell. Who got mini-flashlight?"

"I do," said Judy, pulling a flashlight out of her front pocket.

meep . . . "Shine light on clam," said Thudd. "Clam get lotsa light, clam open up."

Judy snapped on the flashlight and

shined it on the clam. It began to open!

"Well, *thank you!*" said Judy as she pulled her leg out.

"I don't know what Burpp is up to," said Andrew. "But we'd better find a place to hide."

They swam deeper into the narrow passageways of the reef. It was a maze with branching paths.

Awk! squawked Burpp. "Roses are red, octopuses are blue, lots of scary things are waiting for you!" *Awk!*

Andrew pointed to a dark crack in the reef wall. It was almost hidden by waving coral fans.

"We can hide here," he said.

Judy wedged herself into the crack. Andrew squeezed in after her.

FLOOOM!

A giant egg, tall as a person, zoomed by the crack. There was a round window at the front of the egg. At the bottom of the egg were two huge metal bird claws. And inside the egg was Burpp.

"The Egg-Mobile is kind of neat!" said Andrew.

"Hey, Burpp!" yelled Soggy Bob. "Ya see anythin' yet?"

Awk! "Not yet," said Burpp. "But I'll find them."

"Ah suspect yer just havin' fun zoomin' around at top speed," said Soggy Bob. "Ah want ya to look into every nook and cranny. Start from the beginnin'!"

Awk! "All right, Boss," squawked Burpp.

FLOOOM!

The Egg-Mobile zoomed past in the opposite direction.

"Listen," said Andrew. "It will take Burpp a long time to look into all the cracks in the reef."

Andrew peeked out into the main passageway. "We can pile up rocks out there," he said. "When Burpp comes zooming through again, maybe the Egg-Mobile will become a *scrambled* Egg-Mobile!

"Then we can use the compass I found to circle back to the Crab-Mobile. We'll sneak up from behind and get the Water Bug."

Judy shook her head. "Another Bug-Brain

special," she said. "What if Burpp sees the wall and just goes over it?"

Andrew scratched his head.

meep . . . "Drewd and Oody pile rocks," said Thudd. "Thudd look for something."

"Thudd," said Andrew, "I can't let you wander around on the reef. You could get eaten by a fish or something."

meep . . . "Thudd not good fish food," said Thudd. "Gotta go!"

Thudd pushed himself out of Andrew's pocket and jumped onto the coral. Even though he was wearing his Bubble Bag, he scrambled away quick as a crab.

STRONG MUSSELS!

Andrew and Judy gathered loose pieces of rock and piled them up in a narrow space between the coral walls. It wasn't long before Andrew felt something poke his ankle.

Andrew turned to see a big pile of shells at his foot. They looked like black clams.

meep . . . "Found 'em!" came a squeak from behind the pile. Thudd was pushing it!

"Thudd!" cried Andrew.

Andrew picked Thudd up and put him back in his pocket. "What have you got there?" he asked.

meep . . . "Mussels!" said Thudd. "Mussel

animal make strong, strong glue. If Egg-Mobile touch mussel glue, Egg-Mobile stick!"

"Wowzers schnauzers!" said Andrew. "Glue that works underwater. I wish I had thought of that!"

meep . . . "Put mussels on top of piled-up rocks," said Thudd. "Mussels spread glue. If Egg-Mobile bump into rocks, Egg-Mobile get stuck!"

Andrew picked up the mussels and placed them on the rock pile.

Long, sticky threads oozed from the mussels and onto the stones. But a few of the mussels didn't seem interested in spreading their glue.

Andrew gathered them up. "I think these guys are sleeping," he said. He put them into one of his pockets.

Andrew and Judy tucked themselves back into the crack in the coral wall and waited.

They didn't have to wait long.

FLOOOM!

CRACK!

AWK! screamed Burpp. "Mayday! May-day!"

"What is goin' on in there, Burpp?" asked Soggy Bob.

Awk! "The Egg-Mobile hit some rocks, Boss," said Burpp. "They weren't here before. It's got to be those Dubble brats."

"Stop flappin' yer beak and get movin'!" yelled Soggy Bob.

Awk! "Can't do it, Boss!" said Burpp. "The Egg-Mobile is stuck!"

"Dagnabit!" said Soggy Bob. "Use them Egg-Mobile claws!"

Awk! "The claws are stuck, too, Boss!" said Burpp.

"Holy moly!" said Andrew. "That mussel glue has really strong muscles!"

Judy rolled her eyes.

"Grrrrr!" growled Soggy Bob. "Keep on tryin'! Ah can't come in there and getcha. Mah underwater suit is in the wash."

Andrew paddled to the edge of the crack, where there was more light. He pulled the old compass out of his pocket and examined it.

Its round face looked like a clock. The outside rim was marked with *N*, *E*, *S*, and *W* for north, east, south, and west. There was an arrow in the middle. No matter how Andrew turned the compass, the arrow always pointed in the same direction.

meep . . . "Arrow of compass always point north," said Thudd. "Arrow of compass is little magnet. Earth is giant magnet cuz it got big, spinning iron lump in middle. Earth magnet pull little compass magnet."

"The compass can help us circle back through the reef," said Andrew.

Andrew turned the compass so that the arrow pointed to the *N.*

"We came from the west," said Andrew. "And we were going east. We need to go south, then west again. That way we can sneak up behind Soggy Bob and get the Water Bug."

"And we'd better hurry," said Judy, "before that dumb parrot gets loose and finds us."

meep . . . "Look!" said Thudd, pointing to a dark hole in the rock wall.

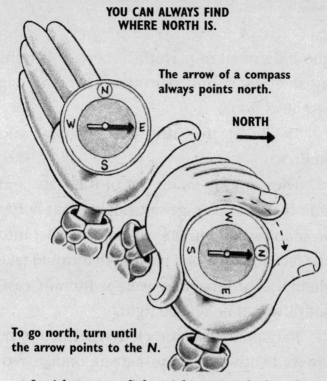

YOU CAN ALWAYS FIND WHERE NORTH IS.

The arrow of a compass always points north.

NORTH →

To go north, turn until the arrow points to the **N**.

Inside was a fish with a purple head and a beak like a bird's. It was stuck inside a gooey bubble.

meep . . . "Parrotfish," said Thudd.

"It's stuck in slime!" said Andrew.

"Let's get it out," said Judy.

"Noop! Noop! Noop!" said Thudd. "Parrotfish make mucus-goo sleeping bag. Mucus

43

goo hide smell of parrotfish. Lotsa fish hunt by smell. Not find parrotfish. Sleeping bag taste bad, too."

"We'll let the little guy snooze," said Andrew.

They quickly swam out of the crack and into the main passageway, hoping that Burpp wouldn't see them. They paddled farther into the reef, looking for a passage that would take them south. Since they were swimming east, south would be on the right.

Judy pointed to a rock that seemed to be covered with dust mops—green, orange, red, and purple! Their frilly threads fluttered as Andrew and Judy swam by.

meep . . . "Animal called sea anemone," said Thudd. "Cousin of jellyfish. Got nasty sting!"

"Look at those pretty little orange fish swimming in the anemones!" said Judy. "*They're* not getting stung."

SEE uh-NEM-uh-nee

meep . . . "Clownfish!" said Thudd. "Got coat of mucus goo. Keep anemone sting away."

Plaaap!

Something smacked the top of Andrew's head.

"Andrew!" yelled Judy. "There's a blue-ringed octopus on your head!"

7 FEELING BLUE

"Uh-oh!" said Andrew. He stopped swimming.

"I guess I'd make it angry if I shoved it off," said Judy.

Plaaap!

A blue-ringed octopus flopped onto Judy's face mask. *Plaaap!* Another one plopped onto her shoulder!

"Cheese Louise!" said Judy. "It's raining blue-ringed octopuses!"

meep . . . "Drewd and Oody not move!" said Thudd.

Thudd crept out of Andrew's pocket and

let himself fall to the coral below. He scuttled over to the anemones. He picked up a big red anemone and headed back.

Thudd climbed up Andrew's Bubble Duds until he got to his knee, where one of the octopuses had landed.

Thudd waved the anemone at the octopus. It got up on its legs and moved toward Thudd. But as soon as Thudd touched it with the anemone, it jetted off!

Thudd climbed to Andrew's elbow and shook the anemone at another octopus. It pulled back and sped away.

Thudd jumped over to Judy. He crept up to each octopus and waggled the anemone. The octopuses left in a hurry.

Thudd went back and forth between Andrew and Judy until all the octopuses were gone.

"Thank you, Thudd!" said Judy. She picked him up and held him in front of her face mask. "I'd give you a big kiss if I weren't wearing a face mask and you weren't inside a plastic bag!"

Thudd's face screen went pink.

"Thudd, that was amazing!" said Andrew. "How did you do it?"

Thudd pointed to a little patch of anemones that seemed to be creeping across a rock. Andrew and Judy leaned down to look closer. The anemones were actually stuck to a shell. Small brown claws were moving it along.

"It's a hermit crab," said Judy.

meep . . . "Octopus like to eat hermit crab," said Thudd. "But octopus not like anemone sting. Hermit crab stick anemone on shell to keep octopus away. Drewd and Oody got to put on anemones, too."

They went over to the patch of anemones, carefully plucked up some big ones, and attached them to their Bubble Duds.

"We look totally stupid," said Judy. "The octopuses will be laughing so hard, they won't be able to bite us. Let's get going!"

"Okay," said Andrew. "But I wish I knew why they attacked us."

Andrew and Judy paddled on.

"Look!" said Judy. She pointed to a little herd of sea horses fluttering toward a tunnel on the right. It was the direction Andrew and Judy needed to go, so they followed.

The tunnel opened into a large rocky room. At one end was a heavy iron door. A sign on the door said:

KEEP OUTTA HERE!

THIS MEANS YOU!

SOGGY BOB SLOGGINS

Andrew's mouth fell open.

"He's everywhere!" said Judy.

"We've got to find out what he's up to," said Andrew.

They swam to the door. Andrew unlatched it and pulled it open. It was dark inside.

Judy snapped on the flashlight.

The beam of light showed a big cage made of woven wire.

"Yowzers!" said Andrew.

The cage was filled with octopuses!

SCHOOL IS OUT!

Some of the octopuses were so big their tentacles could stretch across a room. Small, bumpy ones were curled up in corners of the cage. And there were hundreds of blue-ringed octopuses!

A sign above the cage said:

SOGGY BOB'S OCTOPUS SCHOOL

AND PEARL FARM

Inside the cage were life-size dolls. They looked like Andrew and Judy! The dolls were covered with clams and mussels and blue-ringed octopuses.

meep . . . "Octopus smart, smart, smart!" said Thudd. "Got big brain. Can learn lotsa stuff! Soggy Bob teach blue-ringed octopus that Drewd and Oody good to eat. That why octopus attack. Soggy Bob teach octopus other stuff, too. Look!"

Large brown octopuses were opening oysters as big as pizzas. The insides of the oysters' shells glowed with shimmering colors. The octopuses were putting beads inside the oyster shells.

meep . . . "Bead annoy oyster animal!" said Thudd. "Like when Drewd get pebble in shoe. Oyster cover bead with pearly stuff. Same stuff oyster use to cover inside of shell. Make pearl!"

One of the octopuses opened an oyster. Another octopus watched. Then it picked up an oyster and did the same thing.

meep . . . "Octopus learn from other octopus."

In another corner of the cage, octopuses were opening oysters, taking pearls out, and putting them in buckets. Then they gobbled down the oysters!

The blue-ringed octopuses were gathering at the front of the cage. Their slitty little eyes watched Judy and Andrew. Their blue rings were glowing.

"We don't want to hurt you, little buddies," said Andrew. "And we don't think you really want to attack us, either. So calm down."

Judy shook her head. "Soggy Bob shouldn't be using the octopuses like this," she said.

Andrew nodded. "Maybe we can set them free if we get the Water Bug back," he said.

More and more octopuses were gathering by the door to the cage.

Suddenly a tentacle reached through the cage and lifted the door latch. The door flung open, and a flood of octopuses rushed out!

Judy flattened herself against the sand. "The anemones will protect us, right?" she asked.

"Eek!" yelped Thudd. "Too many octopus! Not enough anemones! Go fast, fast, fast!"

Andrew and Judy paddled furiously.

Most of the octopuses jetted away. But a crowd of blue-ringed octopuses followed them.

"Over here!" said Judy. She squeezed into a crack in the coral wall. The edges of the wall were covered with anemones. Andrew hurried in after her.

The octopuses gathered outside. They looked in, but they wouldn't pass the anemones. They waved their tentacles and jetted off.

When Andrew and Judy hadn't seen any blue-ringed octopuses for a while, they crept out.

"Whew!" said Andrew. "I think they're gone."

"At least we haven't run into any of those sea wasp jellyfish," said Judy.

Andrew scratched his head. "Uncle Al was trying to warn us about one more thing," he said. "I wonder what it was."

meep . . . "Lotsa danger near Great Barrier Reef," said Thudd. He pointed to his face screen. "Got lionfish."

meep . . . "Lionfish got lotsa poison spines on back. Scorpionfish got poison spines, too," said Thudd.

Thudd's screen blinked and showed a fish

that looked like a pile of gray rags.

"That's *not* a good-looking fish," said Judy. "What raggedy lips."

meep . . . "Little fish see scorpionfish lips. Think *food*! Try to bite lips! Scorpionfish gobble up little fish."

"I haven't seen any lionfish or scorpionfish," said Andrew. "But look at these beautiful shells!"

lionfish

scorpionfish

Andrew swooped down to grab a shell. It was shaped like an ice cream cone with pretty brown zigzags. Suddenly there were lots and lots of shells. They were crawling along the sand. They were dive-bombing off the rocky walls—onto Andrew and Judy!

9 ATTACK OF THE CONES

"Eek!" squeaked Thudd. "Not touch! Not touch!"

"Cheese Louise!" said Judy. "Don't get your shorts in a knot, Thudd. It's just some silly little snails."

meep . . . "Cone snail!" squeaked Thudd. "Got tongue with tooth on end. Like harpoon! Snail shoot tooth into prey animal. Tooth got lotsa poison! Strong, strong, strong!"

"Aaaack!" said Judy. She started turning underwater somersaults to keep the snails off.

"Yaaargh!" said Andrew. He shook himself

like a wet dog to get rid of the snails.

Suddenly Thudd's big purple button sprang open. The purple beam zoomed out with the hologram of Uncle Al at the end of it.

"Hey, guys!" said Uncle Al. He was smiling, but his eyes looked worried. "It's been hard to reach you. Are you okay? At least you're back in the Water Bug."

"Um, sorry, Uncle Al," said Andrew, spinning like a top. "Soggy Bob captured the Water Bug. Now we're hiding inside the reef. But we're going to sneak back and get the Water Bug."

"Harry Potter on a ham sandwich!" said Uncle Al. "You kids are danger magnets! Could you please try to be a little bit boring? You'd be safer. . . . You haven't seen any more blue-ringed octopuses, have you? Or sea wasp jellyfish? Or snails with beautiful shells? I didn't get a chance to warn you about the cone snails."

"Um," muttered Andrew, squirming like a nervous worm, "we *did* get attacked by blue-ringed octopuses. Soggy Bob trained them to attack us. We haven't seen any sea wasps, but—"

"But," interrupted Judy, doing backflips, "we're getting mobbed by cone snails!"

Judy saw an umbrella-shaped coral ahead and dragged Andrew under it.

"That's stranger than penguins on bicycles!" said Uncle Al. "Cone snails are usually very shy. They sit in the sand and suck in water through their mouth tube."

meep . . . "Called siphon!" said Thudd.

"The taste of the water tells them if a little fish or worm is close. Then—"

Judy interrupted. "Then the snail shoots out a harpoon tooth filled with poison. We know. Thudd already told us."

Uncle Al rubbed his chin.

"There *is* something that can make snails

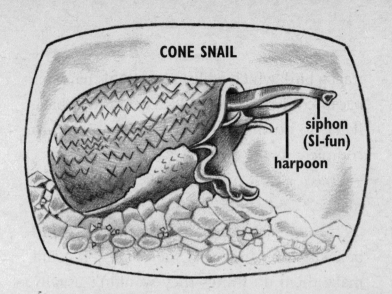

CONE SNAIL

siphon
(SI-fun)

harpoon

do weird things," said Uncle Al. "It's when creatures called parasites get inside them. For example, snails that live on land stay in dark, damp places. They like to be wet and they need to hide from birds that eat snails. But when a certain kind of tiny parasite gets into a snail, it takes over the snail's body and brain."

meep . . . "Brown snail turn lotsa bright colors," said Thudd. "Snail go out into sun! Flash colors!"

Uncle Al nodded. "The flashing colors attract a bird, which will eat it. All this happens because the parasite needs to get inside a bird. It has to do that to make more parasites, to complete its life cycle."

meep . . . "Cone snail got weird parasite, maybe," said Thudd.

"Yup," said Uncle Al. "The parasite could be taking over their tiny snail brains. It could make them do things they wouldn't usually do, like attack people!"

"Euw!" said Judy. "I don't want to be part of anything else's disgusting life cycle."

"Hmmm . . . ," murmured Uncle Al. "Two things that keep snails away are marigold flowers and onions."

"Oh *great*!" said Judy. "Like we have a garden down here!"

"Super-duper pooper-scooper!" said Andrew, reaching into a pocket of his Bubble Duds.

He pulled out a pile of soggy onions.

"These onions are from a pizza you left in the refrigerator of the Water Bug," said Andrew. "But I don't like onions. So I put them in my pocket."

Judy rolled her eyes. "Andrew, you are the sloppiest person in the universe!"

Uncle Al's eyes lit up. "Sometimes a little sloppiness is just what you need," he said. "Rub yourselves with the onions."

Andrew handed Judy half of his onions, and they rubbed them on their Bubble Duds.

The cone snails waved their tube mouths through the water. Then they began to creep away.

"They're leaving!" said Judy.

Uncle Al smiled. "I've told you before. You have everything you need in your heads and in your pockets!"

"Are you almost finished with the See Horse?" asked Judy impatiently.

The See Horse was a new underwater

vehicle Uncle Al was building. He was going to use it to find Andrew and Judy and help them save the giant squids.

"I had a problem with the Nose-O-Matic," said Uncle Al. "It's a new, improved Super-Sniffer. But I think I've got the nose licked."

"Well, hurry up!" said Judy. "This stupid coral reef is scary and dangerous!"

Uncle Al nodded. "I'll be there just as soon as—"

kk . . . kkk . . . kkkkk . . .

"Uh-oh!" said Andrew.

10 CLOWN TO THE RESCUE!

The hologram of Uncle Al stretched like an elastic band, snapped, and disappeared.

Clack! Clack! Clack!

The blue-green water turned dark. A shadow fell over the reef canyon. It was the Crab-Mobile!

The canyon was pretty wide where Andrew and Judy were. The Crab-Mobile might be able to squeeze in!

"Ya little water monkeys are causin' big mischief down there!" came Soggy Bob's gruff voice. "Mah Egg-Mobile is on the rocks, mah octopuses are on the loose, and mah snails are confused! Ah'm comin' to getcha! Heh! Heh! Heh!"

Andrew and Judy swam faster.

Ahead of them, long strands of leafy brown seaweed were swaying.

"Let's duck in there," said Judy.

"It's an underwater forest!" said Andrew as they paddled into the leathery leaves. The long brown stems felt like rubber hoses. The seaweed went up through the water as far as they could see.

meep . . . "Giant kelp!" said Thudd. "Big seaweed! Grow fast, fast, fast! Grow two feet in day! Drewd and Oody eat lotsa giant kelp."

"No *way*!" said Judy. "I would *never* eat seaweed."

meep . . . "Seaweed in ice cream," said Thudd. "Milk shake. Pudding. Lotsa sauce, too!"

"Yuck-a-rama!" said Judy.

"If it tastes good, I'll eat it," said Andrew.

meep . . . "Strange, strange, strange!" said Thudd. "Giant kelp not like to grow here. Water too warm. Someone put giant kelp here."

"Whatever," said Judy. She shoved the stems aside and swam ahead. Andrew followed. The seaweed forest was so thick Andrew couldn't see Judy in front of him.

"Ugh!" yelled Judy. "They're so icky!"

Andrew scrambled through the giant kelp to a circle of open water. In the middle, Judy was kicking her legs and flapping her arms like a big bird.

"What's going on?" asked Andrew.

"It's the sea wasp jellyfish!" yelled Judy.

"I don't see anything," said Andrew.

"That's because they're *transparent*, Bug-Brain!" said Judy. "But I can feel them. They're all squishy and icky. And look!"

She pointed to a sign hanging on the seaweed:

meep . . . "Bubble Duds protect Oody," said Thudd. "But Drewd got big problem."

Thudd pointed to Andrew's foot. It was exposed where the Crab-Mobile had torn away the Bubble Duds.

Judy pushed her way through the sea wasps and swam over to Andrew.

"We don't have any more Bubble Duds patches to cover your foot," she said.

A little orange clownfish swimming through a bright pink anemone caught Judy's eye.

"Wait a minute!" she said. "Clownfish are covered with mucus that keeps them from getting stung by anemones. Anemones sting like jellyfish."

Judy leaned over the anemone. She opened her hands slowly, then quickly grabbed the clownfish.

"Got him!" she said.

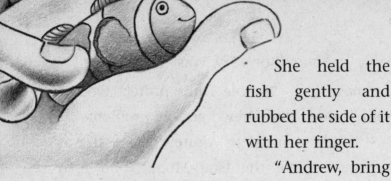

She held the fish gently and rubbed the side of it with her finger.

"Andrew, bring your foot up here," she said.

Judy took the mucus goo she had rubbed off the fish and spread it onto Andrew's foot.

"This might work," she said.

Judy looked at the little clownfish. "You've got plenty of goo left, little fella!" She put him back into his anemone.

Judy pulled Andrew's arm. "Come on, Bug-Brain," she said.

They made their way through the swarm of sea wasps. The jellyfish were hard to see, but Andrew felt the soft, Jell-O-ey blobs as he paddled through.

Then he felt tentacles wrap around his foot!

11 BYE-BYE, BOB!

Andrew held his breath, but all he felt was a little tickle.

Andrew and Judy got to the far side of the sea wasp corral and pushed through the giant kelp. They were in a narrow part of a coral canyon.

It was getting dark. Nighttime was coming.

Above them, Andrew could see the shadow of the Crab-Mobile. It was towing the Water Bug and the cage of sharks.

In the craggy walls around them, parrotfish were tucked into mucus-goo sleeping bags. A huge octopus was stuffed into a cave.

It looked more like a lumpy rock than a live animal, but its slitty eyes were watching them.

Suddenly Andrew had an idea. He pulled the pink and purple anemones off his Bubble Duds and placed them gently on some flat rocks.

"Andrew!" yelled Judy. "What are you *doing*?"

Slowly, the octopus curled a tentacle toward one of Andrew's pockets. It was the pocket where Andrew had put the sleeping mussels.

Andrew moved away. The tentacle wiggled in Andrew's direction, but the octopus stayed in its cave.

Andrew pulled the mussels out of his pocket. "Maybe there's enough," he said. "Come on, Judy. Take off your anemones and let's get the Water Bug."

"Are you *nutso*?" said Judy. "We don't

have anything to protect us from those awful Crab-Mobile claws or to cut the Water Bug loose."

Andrew smiled. "Oh yes, we do," he said.

Andrew paddled higher in the water and wagged the mussels. The octopus twirled its tentacles toward Andrew's hand. Andrew swam higher and dangled the mussels out of the octopus's reach.

"Here, octopus, octopus, octopus!" said Andrew.

The octopus jetted out of its cave. Andrew scrambled up toward the surface. He could feel rubbery tentacles poking at his back. One of them wrapped itself around his ankle!

Andrew came up behind the Crab-Mobile. He stuck some mussels onto the cord of the No-Go Yo-Yo. Then he stuck some onto the giant suction cup.

Andrew crossed his fingers and hoped the mussels were sticky enough to stay.

The octopus let go of Andrew's leg and flung itself at the mussels on the cord.

"Judy!" yelled Andrew to his cousin just below. "Quick! Get into the Water Bug!"

Andrew dove under the Water Bug. Judy was already there. They pressed the buttons on the bottom of the Water Bug seats.

FLAMP!

The seats flipped out. Andrew and Judy belted themselves in, pressed the buttons on the sides of the seats, and flipped themselves inside.

glurp . . . "I tried to escape," said the Water Bug. "I wanted to rescue you. But the suction cup kept my hood shut."

"It's okay," said Andrew.

Outside, the octopus was chomping the mussels. It chewed right through the cord. The Water Bug was free!

Then the octopus slapped itself onto the hood and munched off the mussels and the suction cup.

Soggy Bob must have felt the cord come

loose from the Crab-Mobile. He turned around and his mouth fell open in surprise.

kk . . . kkk . . . kkkkk . . . crackled the speaker.

"I'll be gol-durned!" said Soggy Bob.

Andrew pressed the Octo-Tool button. "Octo-Tool inside!" he said.

"What are you *doing*?" yelled Judy.

"You'll see," said Andrew.

The Octo-Tool tentacles squeezed in through the rubber door under the steering wheel.

Andrew put a mussel in each tentacle.

"Toss the mussels on top of the Crab-Mobile dome!" he ordered. "Quick!"

The tentacles scurried out. They pelted the Crab-Mobile with mussels. The giant octopus flung itself toward the Crab-Mobile and plopped itself down on its glass dome!

"What in tarnation is goin' on here?" growled Soggy Bob.

Clack! Clack! Clack!

The Crab-Mobile claws snapped at the octopus. The octopus wrapped its tentacles around the claws!

Suddenly the octopus jetted backward and downward—taking the Crab-Mobile with it!

kk . . . kkk . . . kkkkk . . .

"Grrrrrrr!" came Soggy Bob's horrible growl through the speakers. "Ya bad, bad water babies better watch out! Ah'll be comin' to getcha!"

It was dark now. Andrew snapped on the Water Bug's headlights. They watched the Crab-Mobile disappear into the gloomy ocean below.

"Wowzers!" said Andrew. He pulled his Bubble Duds helmet off his head.

"Yay!" yelled Judy. She took off her helmet, too.

Andrew turned to Judy. "You know what time it is?" he asked.

"It's pretty late," said Judy.

"It's time to find the giant squids!" said Andrew.

Judy rolled her eyes. "I guess so," she said.

Andrew pressed the silver button that turned on the Super-Sniffer.

"Search for giant squids!" said Andrew into the microphone.

A compass appeared in the middle of the steering wheel. The word *squid* lit up in green letters at the top.

glurp . . . "When the arrow points to *squid*," said the Water Bug, "you are going in the right direction. This will be an interesting trip!"

Andrew turned the steering wheel until the black arrow on the compass pointed to *squid*.

The Water Bug began to dive into the black nighttime ocean. Strangely, the water twinkled with light, like a sky full of stars.

"What's that?" asked Judy, pointing ahead.

Huge roundish, shadowy shapes were swooping toward them.

Uh-oh, thought Andrew. *Those couldn't be flying saucers, could they?*

TO BE CONTINUED IN ANDREW, JUDY, AND
THUDD'S NEXT EXCITING ADVENTURE:

ANDREW LOST
IN THE DEEP!

In stores July 2004

TRUE STUFF

Thudd wanted to tell you more about the strange creatures of the Great Barrier Reef, but he was too busy finding mussels and getting rid of blue-ringed octopuses. Here's what Thudd wanted to say:

• Fishermen used to spread huge nets, miles long sometimes, to catch fish like tuna. These nets trapped other animals, too, including dolphins, whales, seals, and even seabirds. These nets are forbidden now. But many of them drifted to the bottom of the sea and are still dangerous to animals that accidentally swim into them.

• Glass is made of the same stuff as sand. If you heat sand to a very high temperature, it becomes liquid and transparent. When the melted sand cools, it becomes glass!

• "Mayday" is a signal used in emergencies. It comes from the French word *m'aider* (pronounced just like "Mayday"). *M'aider* means "help me."

• The shells of giant clams close too slowly for someone to get a foot caught while just passing by. Judy must have been resting on the giant clamshell while she was waiting for Andrew!

• The skin of giant clams can be many different colors. That's because of the little plants called algae (AL-jee) that live inside the skin. The clam provides a protected place for these tiny plants to live, and the plants help make food for the clam.

• Scientists think the very center of the earth is a giant core of solid super-hot iron. Around the solid iron is a layer of melted iron. This layer spins around slowly. The spinning is what creates the earth's magnetism.

And it's why compasses work!

• Mussels use their powerful underwater glue to anchor themselves to rocks. Scientists are trying to adapt this sticky stuff to use in wet places, like cementing teeth into mouths and joining broken bones together.

• Besides making mucus cocoons, parrotfish have another special ability. Female parrotfish can become male parrotfish!

• The stinging cells of jellyfish look like tiny hooks at the end of a fishing line. Each cell is so small that it would take a hundred of them to cover the period at the end of this sentence. When a jellyfish stings, millions of these microscopic barbs jab into a creature's skin and inject their poison.

• There *is* a skin cream made from clownfish mucus! Swimmers rub it on to keep jellyfish from stinging!

Find out more!

Visit www.AndrewLost.com.

WHERE TO FIND MORE TRUE STUFF

Want to find out about the amazing and mysterious things that can happen in the underwater world? Read these books!

• *Dolphin Adventure* by Wayne Grover (New York: HarperTrophy, 1990). This is the true story of how a family of dolphins asked humans for help to save their injured baby!

• *Shark Lady: True Adventures of Eugenie Clark* by Ann McGovern (New York: Scholastic, 1987) and *Adventures of the Shark Lady: Eugenie Clark Around the World* by Ann McGovern (New York: Scholastic, 1998). In these books, a nine-year-old girl who loves to watch the fish in her aquarium grows up to study sea creatures all over the world. She swims with flashlight fish, rides a monster whale shark, and gets caught in the claws of a giant spider crab!

• *Eyewitness: Ocean* by Miranda Macquitty (New York: DK Publishing, 2000). Lots of information and great pictures tell the story of the oceans—how they were made, what lives in them, and how we explore them.

• *Oceans* by Seymour Simon (New York: HarperCollins Children's Books, 1997). You'll feel the waves when you see these pictures! Lots of great information, too. For example, there are 100 billion gallons of water in the ocean for each person on earth!

• *The Octopus: Phantom of the Sea* by Mary M. Cerullo (New York: Cobblehill Books/Dutton, 1997). Want to find out more about octopuses, including how smart they are and the tricks they play on humans? Read this!

• *Sea Jellies: Rainbows in the Sea* by Elizabeth Tayntor Gowell (London: Franklin Watts, 1993). Jellyfish aren't fish. They don't have hearts or brains or bones, but they hunt and eat and reproduce. They can be smaller than your fingernail or bigger than a washing machine. You can find out how these blobby creatures live and see lots of them in this book.

Turn the page
for a sneak peek at
Andrew, Judy, and Thudd's
next exciting adventure—

ANDREW LOST
IN THE DEEP!

Available July 2004

1 NIGHT LIGHTS

Ten-year-old Andrew Dubble drove deeper and deeper into the ink-dark ocean. In the headlights, he could see huge dishy shapes swooping closer and closer.

Those couldn't *be flying saucers,* he thought. *We're underwater, so they'd have to be* swimming *saucers!*

The flying-saucer shapes were in front of the Water Bug's headlights. The shapes had mouths that were open wide.

"Cheese Louise!" said Judy. "What *are* those things? Their mouths are big enough to swallow us!"

meep . . . "Manta ray!" said Thudd, the little silver robot in the front pocket of Andrew's underwater suit. "Manta ray not eat people. Just eat tiny stuff. Manta mouth like big net."

Judy frowned. "That's what you said about the whale, Smarty-Pants," she said.

Little bursts of bright blue light exploded around the Water Bug. The manta rays tumbled around the Water Bug, gobbling up the mini-fireworks.

"Wowzers!" said Andrew. "What's going on out there?"

meep . . . "Light come from animals with light inside," said Thudd. "Called bioluminescence. Mean 'living light.' Living light help animals find same kind of animal for mate. Find prey to eat. Scare hungry predator, too. Like big camera flash in face! Ocean got lotsa living light. Look!" said Thudd, pointing outside.

As far as they could see, the endless dark

ocean twinkled with a zillion tiny lights.

Suddenly the manta rays flapped away into the glittering blackness like a flock of flying carpets.

Beyond the headlights of the Water Bug, Andrew made out a strange shape coming toward them.

"Wowzers schnauzers!" said Andrew as it came closer. "It looks like a swimming chain saw!"

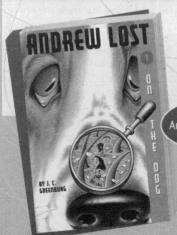

A STEPPING STONE BOOK™

**Great stories by great authors . . .
for fantastic first reading experiences!**

Grades 1–3

FICTION

Duz Shedd series
by Marjorie Weinman Sharmat
Junie B. Jones series by Barbara Park
Magic Tree House® series
by Mary Pope Osborne
Marvin Redpost series by Louis Sachar
Mole and Shrew books
by Jackie French Koller
Tooter Tales books by Jerry Spinelli

The Chalk Box Kid
by Clyde Robert Bulla
The Paint Brush Kid
by Clyde Robert Bulla
White Bird by Clyde Robert Bulla

NONFICTION

Magic Tree House® Research Guides
by Will Osborne and
Mary Pope Osborne

Grades 2–4

A to Z Mysteries® series by Ron Roy
Aliens for . . . books
by Stephanie Spinner & Jonathan Etra
Julian books by Ann Cameron
The Katie Lynn Cookie Company series
by G. E. Stanley
The Case of the Elevator Duck
by Polly Berrien Berends
Hannah by Gloria Whelan
Little Swan by Adèle Geras
The Minstrel in the Tower
by Gloria Skurzynski

Next Spring an Oriole
by Gloria Whelan
Night of the Full Moon
by Gloria Whelan
Silver by Gloria Whelan
Smasher by Dick King-Smith

CLASSICS

Dr. Jekyll and Mr. Hyde
retold by Stephanie Spinner
Dracula retold by Stephanie Spinner
Frankenstein retold by Larry Weinberg

Grades 3–5

FICTION

The Magic Elements Quartet
by Mallory Loehr
Spider Kane Mysteries
by Mary Pope Osborne

NONFICTION

Balto and the Great Race
by Elizabeth Cody Kimmel
The *Titanic* Sinks!
by Thomas Conklin